Mites
to
Mastodons

A Book of Animal Poems

Maxine Kumin ● **Illustrated by Pamela Zagarenski**

Edited by Liz Rosenberg

Houghton Mifflin Company   Boston 2006

www.houghtonmifflinbooks.com

The text of this book is set in Aged, American Typewriter, Aunt Mildred,
Korinna, Caecilia, Clearface, Officina, Regula, Shannon, and Simoncini Garamond.
The cover display type is Triplex.

The illustrations are mixed media on paper, canvas, and wood;
collage, and computer graphics.

Library of Congress Cataloging-in-Publication Data

Kumin, Maxine, 1925–
Mites to mastodons : a book of animal poems / by Maxine Kumin ;
illustrated by Pamela Zagarenski, edited by Liz Rosenberg.
p. cm.
ISBN-13: 978-0-618-50753-5 (hc)
ISBN-10: 0-618-50753-1 (hc)
1. Animals—Juvenile poetry. 2. Children's poetry, American.
I. Zagarenski, Pamela. II. Title.
PS3521.U638M58 2006
811'.54—dc22   2004018777

Manufactured in China
SCP 10 9 8 7 6 5 4 3 2 1

To Liz, who made it happen
—M.K.

I dedicate this book to all who hold it
in their hands . . . tall and small
—P.J.Z.

Mites

You have to have eight legs to be
counted in the spider family.

This tiny creature, seen up close
through the lens of a magnifying glass,

with his yellow spots and a sprinkling of spines,
absolutely fits the design

of a two-spotted mite, who eats whatever
it finds with its fangs, which are sharp and clever.

Spinach is nice, and so is corn in a plot,
and houseplants. Mites also like roses a lot.

But remember, the two-spotted mite is so small
that you might at first glance see nothing at all

but a fuzzy white leaf in a flowerpot,
till you look through a lens at moving dots,

crunching and munching all in one spot,
millions and millions of moving dots.

Inchworm

Think about the inchworm,
  inching on the grass.
Inchmeal the inchworm
  waits for ants to pass.

He feels his way at corners.
He looks down every road,
  afraid to make an inch meal
  for a hopping toad.

I think about the inchworm,
  who travels inch by inch.
When I walk a mile to town,
  my shoes begin to pinch.

Does his bottom bother him,
  inching up a stalk?
An inch for an inchworm
  is a morning's walk.

Snail

No one writes a letter to the snail.
He does not have a mailbox for his mail.
He does not have a bathtub or a rug.
There's no one in his house that he can hug.
There isn't any room when he's inside.
And yet they say the snail is satisfied.

Polliwogs

Salamanders, toads, and frogs
all begin as polliwogs
hatching out in swampy bogs.

Polliwogs begin as eggs,
first sprout tails and, later, legs.
Eggs are laid by mother frogs,

who began as polliwogs.

Owl

My favorite barred owl, who lives in the woods
    nearby, wakes me, hooting, "Who cooks for you-u-u?"
And if I could hoot I'd answer, "I do-oo-oo
    but I wish you could, you could, you could."

He is up all night, my owl, and like others roosts in a tree
    or a barn all day, where nobody else can see.

When he wakes, the owl preens, yawns, and combs his head
    with his beak. He cleans his claws and toes with his beak.
And he doesn't just hoot. Sometimes he purrs instead,
    or whistles, screeches, snorts, chitters, and hisses to speak

owl to owl. Next time, in the dark, take your friend's hand
    and listen hard. How much owl talk can you two understand?

Squirrel

Guess who is everyone's acrobat?
Guess who can use his great bushy tail
as a rudder whenever he springs like a cat
from high branch to rooftop? Our backyard gray squirrel.

He wraps himself up in his tail when it's cold.
In summer it serves as his parasol.
When he chatters he thrashes his tail to scold
—or is it to praise?—beings large and small.

His cousins include the smaller red squirrel
and everyone's favorite, the orange and brown
chipmunk, who seeks little nooks in stone walls
for a bedroom when winter spreads snow all around.

What do squirrels eat? In spring, the green shoots
of maples; in summer, small fruits and berries;
but year round, saved up, it's all kinds of NUTS.
The more nuts a squirrel has, the fewer his worries.

Rabbit

This fellow's feelings will not be hurt
  if dinner is served without dessert.

Nobody has to tell him to finish
  his beans, asparagus, peas, or spinach.

Nobody needs to wait while he eats
  his Brussels sprouts or cabbage or beets.

And when they ask him he always says yes
  to seconds of turnips or watercress.

Cats

When I grow up, I plan to keep
eleven cats, and let them sleep
on any bedspread that they wish,
and feed them people's tuna fish.

Pekinese

How cuddly is the Pekinese
upon his silken pillow.
You need to say, "Excuse me, please"
before you pat this fellow.

Before you stroke his coat of fluff
or touch his tiny ankle
you'd better ask permission of
his mom and dad and uncle.

Anteater

For lunch and for dinner, nothing is sweeter
  than termites and ants to the giant anteater,
  who flicks his tongue out to capture his prey
  faster than clocks tick the minutes away.

He also finds soft-bodied grubs attractive.
His two-foot-long tongue is remarkably active.
It traps thirty thousand insects a day,
  zipping out, zipping in, in a lightning-quick way.

You may think his diet is far from yummy,
  but that's what goes into the
anteater's tummy.

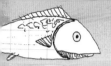

Octopus

The octopus, an ocean creature,
　was oddly engineered by nature

　　with a bulbous, floppy head, big eyes,
　　and suction cups that line both sides

　　of its eight arms, which means it can
　　hold fast to lobsters, crabs, and clams.

When attacked, it shoots a screen
　of blackest ink, then leaves the scene.

It changes color to fit its mood:
　when frightened, white; when angry, red.

Most of the time it's simply brown
　to match the ocean floor's background.

The plural, when there's more than one,
　is *octopi*. When fully grown

　　they range from tiny—half an inch—
　　to ones who could eat you for lunch:

　　fifteen feet long, thirty feet across,
　　a hundred pounds of octopus.

Still, octopi can squeeze inside
　the smallest crevices to hide.

Their bodies are so soft that they
　can tuck themselves safely away.

You will agree that none of us
　can change shape like the octopus.

Alligator

Old bull of the waters,
old dinosaur cousin,
with scales by the hundreds
and teeth by the dozen,

old singer of swamplands,
old slithery swimmer,
what do you dream of
when fireflies glimmer?

Can you remember
the folktales of old
when you breathed fire
and guarded the gold,

and stole lovely ladies
and captured their kings,
and flew over mountains
on magical wings?

Old bull of the waters,
how can you know
that men made you a dragon,
in dreams, long ago?

Kangaroo

When the kangaroo baby, a joey, is born,
he looks like a little pink lima bean.

He worms his way up his mother's fur,
dives into her pouch, and stays in there,

sucking milk from her teat till he's grown into
    a full adolescent-size kangaroo.

He's almost too big to wiggle his way
    out of the pouch on that special day

    when he's ready to hop—thirty feet in one leap—
    with the rest of the mob, which is what a group

    of 'roos is known as, down under, in
    Australia, a separate continent,

    a magical land where marsupials
    hop at high speeds with their muscular tails,

    live on grasses and leaves and roots, and chew
    their cuds the same way our cows and goats do.

Oh, to be a kangaroo!

Polar Bear

A polar bear need not think twice
before he slides downhill on ice.

Nothing gives him four cold feet,
a runny nose, a chilly seat.

Sometimes, to travel back and forth
fishing in the frozen north,

he hitches rides on iceberg peaks
and drifts along for weeks and weeks.

Manatee

You'll have to go to Florida to see
the bulgy creature called the manatee.

Shaped like an overweight seal, it swims about
with two front flippers and a whiskery snout

and a quite useful tail that sets the pace
by paddling so leisurely in place

that algae clumps have ample time to grow
along its undersides. These gentle, slow

creatures graze along the ocean floor
for food and can live sixty years or more.

Who are their closest relatives?
You'll find this stunning to believe:

It's not the lion, mouse, or ant.
The answer is the elephant.

Manatees and elephants
had the same ancestor once.

Millions of years of evolution
led to this bizarre solution:

The manatee stayed warm and wet.
The elephant climbed out to get

four feet, a trunk, and grew to be
the largest land mammal in history.

Big as they are, let's be aware
that both of them need human care.

Camel

The camel's a mammal
that grouches and grumps.
I think that he wishes
he didn't have humps.

Giraffe

You must not laugh at the giraffe.
Even on stilts, you're less than half
   as tall as he. His rosy tongue
   is more than eighteen inches long.

He feeds on treetops' leafy tips,
   where no one else can reach, except
   for elephants, whose trunks can stretch
   as high as the giraffes' slim necks.

His eyesight is so sharp that he
   can spot you half a mile away.
To drink, he either must fold down
   his forelegs or straddle the edge of the pond.

They are not silent. The babies mew
   and bleat the way tame cows' calves do.
These are the facts. Please do not laugh
   at the world's tallest mammal, our giraffe.

Extinct

X stands for **eXtinct**, I'm sorry to say.
Thousands of creatures have faded away.

Tyrannosauruses, tough wooly mammoths,
   and others whose names you don't know have vanished:

   the Labrador duck, the central hare wallaby,
   the black-footed ferret, the burrowing betony,

   the heath hen, the great auk, the New Zealand quail,
   the bandicoot, sea mink, Arabian gazelle,

Tasmanian tiger, and giant fruit bat.
The list of the vanished is longer than that,

   but let's all look after the mammals and birds
   and reptiles and fish that are left here. The word

we need to remember, that makes us think,
   that almost begins with **X**, is **eXtinct.**

Mastodon

The mastodon
  didn't need to put anything else on.
His shaggy coat
  struck exactly the right wintry note
  twenty million years ago.
Back then
  he roamed a colder world of ice and snow,
  before women
  or men, great apes, or dogs or even guinea pigs
  were known.

The mastodon
  browsed through northern forests, nipping twigs
  and leaves
  with special pointed teeth. He left his bones
  in sandy graves
  for archaeologists to come upon
  along the shores
  of lakes Ontario, Superior, Huron,
  Erie, and Michigan.

He was the ancestor
  of our own elephant, the largest beast
  on earth today. Oh, what a feast
  it would have been, those million years ago,
  to spy the herd galloping through falling snow.

Imagine them: ten tons
  of thundering mastodons!

See you later . . .